──IN **MINNESOTA**

Sue Carabine

Illustrations by
Shauna Mooney Kawasaki

Gibbs Smith, Publisher

First Edition
12 11   9 8 7 6

Published by
Gibbs Smith, Publisher
P.O. Box 667
Layton, Utah 84041

1-800-748-5439 orders
www.gibbs-smith.com

Edited by Linda Nimori
Designed and produced by Mary Ellen Thompson,
 TTA Design
Printed and bound in China

ISBN10: 1-58685-275-2
ISBN13: 978-1-58685-275-7

'Twas the night before Christmas,
Nick was over the quota
Of toys for the kids in
snowy cold Minnesota,

But Nick didn't care,
he was just so elated,
Returning was all
he'd anticipated!

The Mall of America
would be the first stop
'Cause after the Pole,
it's the best place to shop!

Then on to the Mayo
for his yearly check-up,
To make sure his step
was as spry as a pup!

And next he'd deliver
his gifts to the Twins,
The Lynx, and the Vikings
for all their great wins.

Also the Timberwolves
along with the Wild—
Just seeing these athletes again
made him smile.

Now they were nearing
the great Gopher State,
Soaring over the many
blue shimmering lakes.

"Fly closer in, boys,"
Santa called to his deer,
"Some folks there below
need our help around here."

He'd spied several fishermen
down on the ice.
"They must be in trouble
to be fishing tonight!"

As he landed the sleigh,
Nick jumped out, made a hole
In the ice, then grabbed hold
of his own fishing pole.

The guys started talking
and told St. Nick why
They'd not made it home,
although all of them tried.

Together they'd worked
at the job late till finished,
Then tried to get home—
but their hopes soon diminished!

The youngest, named Charlie,
said, "I'm from Duluth,
This year would have been
my first Christmas with Ruth.

"Been married three months,
and my sweet wife was countin'
On Christmas, just us
skiing on Spirit Mountain!

"Well, that's life," Charlie sighed.
"Hey, Nick, you need help!
You won't catch fish that way
even if the ice melts!

"If you watch me close, Santa,
and do it this way,
You'll grill luscious lake trout
at home Christmas Day!"

As Charlie helped Nick,
an old fellow recalled
His plans for this Christmas,
where each, one and all,

Of his family would be there
(aunts, uncles, and cousins);
No matter the journey,
there'd be dozens and dozens!

"Hey, Nick, my hometown is
Minneapolis–St. Paul,
Our wonderful capital,
the home of The Mall.

"It's the first time we've all
been together for years,
And if I'm not there
Jane will soon be in tears!

"Such plans for our grandkids—
the Skyway and IMAX,
Whatever they want
they had only to ask.

"The Children's Museum
and Minnesota Zoo
Were some of the fun things
we wanted to do!

"We're both getting older,
so this could be our last
Yuletide with them, Santa.
I must get home—fast!"

Nick felt a close kinship
with this old curmudgeon,
Was about to respond when
he felt someone nudge him.

"Hi, Santa, I'm Jeff,
what you usin' for bait?
Whatever it is,
it's not workin' real great.

"I've caught three large trout
since you put your line in.
Now, what's goin' on?
Your night crawlers too thin?

"I live in Mankato.
My three kids are there,
I promised I'd get home
with enough time to spare

"For us to go shopping,
sing carols together
In Emerald Green Valley,
whatever the weather!

"They only have me
(there is no one else),
Little Joe and the twins,
we all manage ourselves.

"But, here, let me help you.
May I bait your line?"
Nick smiled, "It's okay,
I can manage just fine!"

The last fellow, Paul,
seemed to be all alone,
Was deep in his thoughts
as he worked on his own.

He was carving on something,
so they all let him be.
Soon Paul held out something
for Santa to see:

A music box wondrous
made by his own hand.
Paul whispered, "St. Nick,
do you know what I'd planned?

"My sweet daughter, Abbey,
is waiting for me
At home in Rochester,
as sick as can be!

"The doc at the Mayo
says she's on the mend,
So carving this box was
good time I could spend.

"But this Christmas Eve
will be over with haste;
I'll not see the sweet smile
on dear Abbey's face."

As he talked, he reached out,
gently pulled on Nick's line,
saw the hook had no bait,
so he said, "Please, use mine."

But Santa just chuckled,
cried, "I've a good reason:
All fish should have fun
at this glorious season!

"And my gift to you men
at this best time of year
Is to get you home safely.
So, grab all your gear,

"And empty your creel
as you 'catch and release,'
Then jump in the sleigh, boys,
we'll fly like wild geese."

Nick's sleigh headed south,
then set down at Duluth,
Charlie rushed to the arms
of his lovely bride, Ruth.

The reindeer then soared
over Aerial Lift Bridge,
Neared an old Viking ship
after topping a ridge.

They continued on down to
Minneapolis–St. Paul,
Left the old gent at home
with his grandkids and all,

Who shrieked with excitement
and called to St. Nick,
"Oh, thank you, dear Santa,
and please come back quick!"

Then, on to Mankato
where Jeff returned home.
(Now Joe and the twins won't
spend Christmas alone.)

They were thrilled to see daddy,
And hugged him so tight.
Jeff gave thanks in his heart
For this wondrous night!

When Nick saw Leed Castle
his white mustache curled!
And the reindeer were giddy
at Underwater World.

Then finally in Rochester
Abbey hugged Dad,
She was so very pleased
with the gift that he had.

There were tears on his cheeks
as Paul tucked her in bed,
And the music box tinkled
As Nick quietly said,

"Merry Christmas, Minnesota—
from Bloomington to Fergus Falls
To Nitty Gritty Granite City—
my best to you all!"